This book belongs to

_____

VOLUME 13

FERDINAND
AND THE BULLIES

WALT DISNEY FUN-TO-READ LIBRARY

ISBN 1-885222-25-4
Advance Publishers Inc., P.O. Box 2607, Winter Park, FL. 32790
Printed in the United States of America
098765432

Most bulls in Spain wanted to fight in the bullring. Ferdinand did not. He liked to sit under his favorite cork tree. He liked to smell the flowers.

He always knew when there was going to be a bullfight in the city. Men came to the pasture then. They came to pick the best fighting bulls.

All the bulls bellowed. They snorted. They pawed the ground. They wanted to be picked.

Ferdinand did not. He sat under his cork tree. He just smelled the flowers.

Each time the men came, they took away one of the bulls in a truck. The rest were sad because they had not been picked. But Ferdinand was not.

After some time, all the bulls that
Ferdinand grew up with had gone off to the
bullring. Now there were younger bulls who
bellowed and snorted. They pawed the ground.
They too wanted to be picked for the bullring.

The young bulls watched Ferdinand as he sat under his cork tree. They made fun of him all day long.

One young bull did not make jokes about Ferdinand. That was his nephew, Ramon.

Ramon liked his uncle. He did not like to
hear the young bullies' jokes.

"Why don't you act like the other bulls,
Uncle Ferdinand?" Ramon asked. "Why do you
let those bullies make fun of you?"

"Any fool can make a lot of noise," Ferdinand told Ramon. "But it takes a strong bull to go his own way and forget the things those bullies say."

And that is what Ramon told the young bullies. "My Uncle Ferdinand could bellow and snort. He could paw the ground if he wanted to. He just does not want to."

The young bullies did not believe that for a minute. They snickered and sneered.

"We will show you that your uncle is no real bull," the young bullies laughed. They pulled up some of Ferdinand's favorite flowers. Then they snorted and pawed the ground.

They got closer and closer to Ferdinand.
He felt sad. He did not like to see the
flowers spoiled.

But Ferdinand did not bellow or snort. He just settled down to sleep under his cork tree.

While Ferdinand slept, the bullies tied his tail to the tree. Then they sneaked off.

Ferdinand woke up. He started to walk
away. But his tail held him fast to the tree.

The bullies watched. "Now we will see if he can bellow and snort!"

Ferdinand did not bellow. Ferdinand did not snort. He just gave a great, big pull. *Swish!* The branch flew through the air.

Then Ferdinand went back to his cork
tree. He smelled the flowers that were left.

But the young bullies would not give up. At one end of the pasture they found a tree covered with vines. They pulled down some long vines.

Then the bullies waited for night.
While Ferdinand slept, the bullies crept
over to him very quietly. They wound the
vines all around him.

In the morning, Ferdinand woke up. He looked down and saw that he was tied up from head to foot.

The young bullies watched him. What would Ferdinand do now?

Ferdinand was angry. But he knew that bellowing and snorting would not help. Quickly he set to work. He chewed through one piece of vine at a time. Soon he was free.

Later that morning, Ramon came over to sit with his uncle. "Those bullies told me about the trick they played on you, Uncle Ferdinand," he said. "Someone should teach them a lesson. Why don't you do it?"

"Yes, Ramon, someone should teach them
a lesson," Ferdinand agreed. "But don't let
them upset you. Forget about their silly tricks.
Let's go get something to eat."

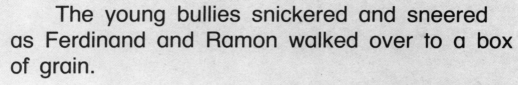

The young bullies snickered and sneered as Ferdinand and Ramon walked over to a box of grain.

Ferdinand took a great mouthful of grain.
"Achoo!" he sneezed. Out flew a mouthful of ants!

That morning, the bullies had left a line of grain from Ferdinand's favorite box right to a nearby anthill. Now Ferdinand's grain was filled with ants.

Slowly Ferdinand turned around. He gave another great sneeze. It sounded like a bellow of rage. He stared at the bullies.

The young bullies backed away. They were afraid.

But Ferdinand did not bellow. He did not snort. He did not paw the ground. He took a deep breath. Then he walked to the pond for a quiet drink.

Now the young bullies decided not to play any more tricks on Ferdinand. Instead, they would pick on Ramon.

"You aren't a real bull, either," they sneered at him.

"I am too a real bull," he cried.

"No, you're not," they shouted.

The bullies gathered together. They made a circle around Ramon. They butted him with their sharp horns.

Poor Ramon was no match for them all. "Help!" he cried.

Ferdinand heard Ramon's cry. He raised his head. He looked around. He saw Ramon. <u>And</u> he saw the bullies.

Ferdinand's eyes flashed. He gave a great snort. He pawed the ground. With a mighty bellow, he ran at the bullies. He butted with his horns. He kicked with his feet.

The young bullies cried out in fear.
They tried to run this way. They tried to
run that way. But Ferdinand was everywhere
at once. The young bullies ran away.

Ferdinand shook his head. He swished his tail. With his head high, he walked back to Ramon.

"Uncle Ferdinand, that was great!" Ramon
said with pride. "I have never seen you get
so angry before!" He started to paw the ground
the way Ferdinand had done.

The young bullies just watched. They were sure to keep far away.

Ferdinand and Ramon walked over to the cork tree.

"A wise bull gets angry only when he must," said Ferdinand. "He only uses his strength to help someone who is really in need."

"Uncle Ferdinand, when I grow up, I want to be just like you," said Ramon.

He settled down with Ferdinand under the cork tree.

And together, they smelled the beautiful flowers.